Dimetrodon

How should you color your dinosaur? Any way you like! You can imagine that it was trying to blend in with the plants or rocks around it and was green or brown. Or, perhaps it was supposed to appear threatening, and was dark and fearsome. Maybe it was even looking for a mate and showed bright colors to attract attention. You decide.

Dimetrodon was a mammal-like reptile which lived in the Permian age, about 280 million years ago. The spines along the back of Dimetrodon probably had skin and blood vessels forming a "solar collector"; this could be turned toward the sun when the creature wanted warmth and away when it did not.

Ornitholestes & Archaeopteryx

Ornitholestes ("bird-robber") lived in Wyoming in the Upper Jurassic period, about 147 million years ago. It was about seven feet long and had strong fingers with claws so that it could easily grab small animals for food. Here it is catching Archaeopteryx ("old wing"), an ancestor of modern birds. Archaeopteryx was about the size of a crow. It probably could not fly, but may have been able to glide.

Hypsilophodon

Hypsilophodon ("high-crested tooth") was probably a very fast runner. It was once thought to live in trees, but scientists now think that it only jumped into trees occasionally, to find food or for protection from its enemies.

Allosaurus

The Allosaurus ("other lizard") was not a friendly beast. It had claws for tearing meat on all four limbs, and its large jaws could make short work of dinner. Allosaurus was large, about 35 feet long, but ate much larger dinosaurs like the brontosaurus.

Elasmosaurus

Elasmosaurus ("thin-plated lizard") lived entirely in the water. Its flippers probably did not move it much faster than a turtle, but it made up for any lack of speed with its amazingly long (23 feet!) neck and sharp teeth, which could snap up fish.

Styracosaurus

Styracosaurus ("spike lizard") had six long spikes around the edge of its skull, enough to discourage almost any enemy. Behind the beak-like tip of its nose was a powerful jaw that could chew up almost any vegetable material.

Stegosaurus

Stegosaurus ("plated lizard") was equipped with a double row of bony plates along its back and large, sharp spines on its tail. The plates are usually thought of as armor, but we do not know exactly how they were used. If they were arranged standing up or lying flat, there would still have been large parts of the animal left unprotected. It is possible that the plates were intended for some purpose other than protection.

Brontosaurus

(Apatosaurus)

Brontosaurus ("thunder lizard") was one of the largest animals ever to walk on land. Its long neck probably developed so that it could reach the tops of tall trees—when a herd of 30-ton Brontosaurs had been in one spot for very long, tree tops were probably all that was left to eat!

Rhamphorynchus was small and light, about the size of a robin, but with a long tail. Its leathery wings were particularly good for gliding.

Pterodactylus

Pterodactylus ("winged finger") had thin, leather-like wings extending from its fourth finger. Its long beak had teeth on both sides, but it was in many ways similar to a modern bird.

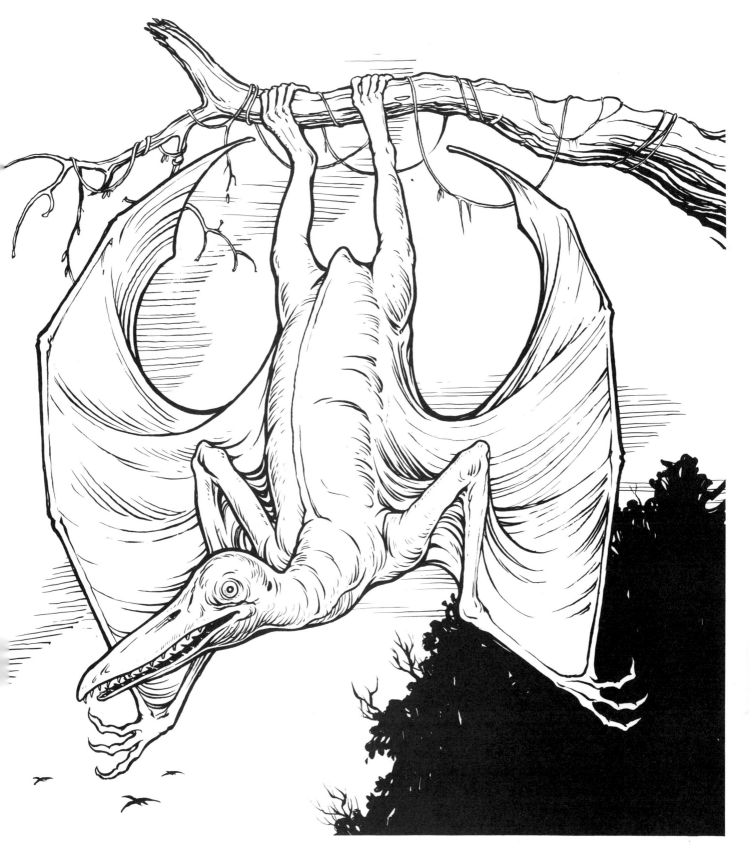

Tyrannosaurus Rex

Tyrannosaurus rex ("king of the tyrant lizards") was the largest meat-eating land animal ever and grew up to 40 feet from head to tail. Its short, weak front legs were probably used mostly for balancing; the four hind toes had talons which could hold onto prey. However, Tryannosaurus rex's greatest weapon was its huge mouth. Its several dozen teeth grew as long as six inches and had serrated edges, "the better to eat you with, my dear."

Ankylosaurus

Ankylosaurus ("curved lizard"), like Stegosaurus, ate small, tender plants. Its armor was rather like an armadillo's, and its head, also armored, could be pulled back inside its shell like a turtle's. If an enemy came too close, Ankylosaurus could do serious damage with the bony "club" at the end of its tail.

Protoceratops

Protoceratops ("first horn face") grew up to eight feet long. Its head was almost as long as its back and had a bony shield covering its neck. Protoceratops lived on plants, which it ground with its mighty jaws.

Hatching of Protoceratops

A mother Protoceratops would dig a hole in the sand, just the way turtles do today, and lay about 15 eggs in it. She probably then covered the eggs with sand and left them to hatch, warmed by the sun's heat. Perhaps the mother returned to raise the young after they had hatched, for they were relatively helpless when small.

Parasaurolophus

Parasaurolophus ("almost crested lizard") was a plant eater which grew to several tons in weight. Its most remarkable feature was the long, hollow bone "crest" which grew out of its head. This bone was connected with its nose and probably gave the animal a very good sense of smell so that it could easily find food or identify enemies.

Triceratops

Triceratops ("three-horned eye") weighed over eight tons and must have galloped rather like a buffalo. Its skull was seven feet long, and its body grew to about thirty feet long and eight feet high. Triceratops could use its horns both to break up the plants on which it fed and to fend off the fierce Tyrannosaurus.

Pteranodon had a 25-foot wingspan and a beak like a pelican's, used to gather fish.

Iguanodon

From its fossilized footprints, we think that Iguanodon ("iguana-tooth")
walked on two legs, but it may have walked on its front legs at times.
Iguanodons grew up to 30 feet long. They ate plants; when their teeth wore
down from chewing, a new row of teeth would grow in.